The Curious Case of
Jacobite Gold

by

R.V.W. JACKSON

Contents

ISBN 9798536154601

****

Other books by the same author:
THE TIME LABORATORY (Feb 2020).
THE OBSERVERS (Mar 2019)
ALGERNON: Radio Ham Extraordinary (May 2017).

Dedication

For Ethan, Luke and Lily.

Acknowledgements

With appreciation for helpful comments from my better half Elizabeth Ann (also an author).

The Curious Case of Jacobite Gold

x

Chapter 1

EIGHT DAYS WITHOUT a computer – and now, here it is. All I have to do is sign the papers and have the trolley wheeled into the laboratory.

'Your lucky day!' our Chief Technician says, looking up from his desk with a smile.

'Great!'

'But you can't take it just yet.'

'Huh?'

'I forgot – you're new here. Our electronics guys have to safety check it first.'

'Oh, all right. How long will that take?'

'There's a slight backlog. Five or six working days.'

'A whole WEEK?' I must sound quite agitated.

'Hey, easy Lucy. It really isn't worth busting a blood vessel over.'

'Then can I watch you check the contents?' I ask.

'Sure.' Joe's craft knife and a practised hand make short work of the seals and wrapping. A large flat screen emerges, followed by the base unit with its mouse and keyboard. I hardly notice the flood of polystyrene beads erupting onto the floor… something else catches my attention. Labels. Several small green labels. I stare incredulously.

'Looks like it's been tested already - through our workshops!' I say.

Joe shrugs, scratches an ear and makes some entries on his tablet. He passes me some transfer documents for countersigning. Within five minutes I have the system fired up on my desk. But it takes me another half-hour to realise that the machine is not quite like the one I'd ordered from the catalogue. Maybe the manufacturers have upgraded the model slightly. There is something different about those safety labels, too. It's the writing - not Jean Sullivan's, like on the other equipment in our lab. Who cares, I think jubilantly. It's certified and running, so here goes...

Curiously, my choice of internet search engine is ignored and the system invokes a totally unfamiliar one. I'm about to click on the screen's *'Back'* command when a voice-over says, *'Hello, Lucy. Welcome to Hyperspan-XL. Our nation-wide information survey has noted your interest in postage stamp collecting. Perhaps we can help. This is not a sales promotion; we are merely pleased to inform you of opportunities – there is no fee, no obligation...'* It carries on in this vein for a few minutes, allowing me to put several questions and coming up with quite useful answers. More, it says, can be found on such-and-such links to various web addresses.

Three weeks into my job as a Research Associate at the University's Department of Computing, my machine crashes. It has to go back to the supplier. How much I miss the dialogues with Hyperspan-XL! Or, more particularly, with Hendrik – the person at the other end looking after me. That's how it seemed at the time. It didn't occur to me until the day before the computer was returned – two weeks later – that I'm the one who is being asked at least as many questions. Not all of them direct, of course. But little by little there must have been enough transfer of information for that Hyperspan-XL guy to have built up a very thorough dossier on all my interests and activities. Not to mention the identities and occupations of many friends and associates. And as if that isn't enough trouble...

The morning the machine arrives back on my desk, Professor Hamilton calls me into his office.

'Lucy, I've been thinking...'

The thought crosses *my* mind: *Well, I suppose that's what professors do, occasionally.* But his next utterance wipes the smile from my face.

'The work we've given you is perhaps not as interesting to you as we'd assumed.'

'Professor?'

'Or rather – as we'd been led to believe from your interview with us.'

'But I…'

'It's clear to both of us that you've spent more time in contact with one internet site than all the others put together. Far be it for me to tell someone of your experience how to conduct research...' The professor rises from his desk and walks to the window. 'But I'm becoming concerned that you might compromise yourself as well as the project, should this pattern continue.'

'I'm sorry. You're right. I was preoccupied,' I confess.

'By the way,' Professor Hamilton continues, 'if you don't mind telling me, what's so special about this web site which holds such fascination for you?' He returns to his desk and begins accessing the internet from his workstation. 'I've forgotten - what's it called, Lucy?'

'Hyperspan-XL.' I reply.

'Okay…' He raises a bushy eyebrow. 'How is it spelled?'

'With a hyphen and dot com on the end,' I say.

'Hm. No such web site,' he says. 'If you don't believe me, try it yourself.'

I do. And draw a blank, even when I try logging in with my own university ID and password.

The professor accompanies me down the stairs, back to my office in the ground floor laboratory. I must seem visibly shaken. I certainly feel so.

'I don't understand it!' I repeat for the fourth or fifth time.

Perhaps his advanced years have immunised him to the niceties of political correctness; his mood changes and I feel a comforting hand on my shoulder. 'Probably gone to the wall, Lucy,' he said. 'These days, most small businesses last only a couple of years. Put it behind you, dear. Think of it as a blessing in disguise and carry on with your research.'

The door closes and I hear his footsteps recede along the corridor and then his distant measured tread on the stairway. The machine is back on my desk and I turn it on to start the day's work.

As the screen lights up, a familiar voice-over is saying, *'Welcome again to Hyperspan-XL, Lucy. I've missed you, but thank you for resuming our little relationship. How may I help you?'*

Below the Hyperspan-XL logo a picture appears. I see myself sitting on a park bench – it's Regent's Park – beside Hendrik. He has his arm around my shoulder, a bizarre parody of the professor's gesture of a few moments ago. I shudder and my stomach feels knotted. I've never been to Regent's Park with Hendrik. It's obviously a put-together picture, probably digitally doctored using my mug-shot on the university department's web page. Clever, though; the faces are turned towards each other and smiling intimately. I reach for the mains plug.

'Don't do that, Lucy.'

I freeze. Okay, all our computers are equipped with a tiny camera. But I haven't issued any commands to activate mine.

'Why shouldn't I? I'm perfectly free to turn you off!' My voice already lacks conviction and I feel all desire to disconnect evaporating.

The picture no longer seems alien and I'm once more overcome by curiosity as to what should happen next. Of course, the professor was right; interest in my research project has totally given way to this new obsession. It's one thing to be told, another to realise it for myself. In a flash it dawns upon me that Hendrik has hijacked my curiosity –

completely. He's become the sole owner of it. I've accepted the carrots – to the benefit of my hobbies: stamp collecting, bargain-travel holidays, aquatic plants and rare books. And in return I've surrendered my will. As these thoughts race through my head, my strength returns. Hendrik must have gathered this from my facial expression.

'I came up with something interesting about science-fiction first editions over the weekend, he says. *But I can see you have work to do – please don't let me intrude. Maybe later…'Bye for now, Lucy.'*

The screen switches abruptly to the university's home page. Hendrik is easing off, just a little. He knew I would be back, and so did I. But inwardly I'm rejoicing at having, at last, some control over his behaviour. Then I feel a wave of uncertainty. Is this another ploy? Our relationship is growing more complex – and hence, perhaps, more intriguing; *captivating* might be a more appropriate word. And the professor, how can I admit to him that I'm still involved? On the other hand, perhaps he'll help me, in spite of his fanatical devotion to research into information processing and involvement with departmental administration.

I suspect the camera has been monitoring my body language. The screen switches back to Hyperspan-XL and Hendrik's rugged but kindly countenance appears in a talking-head box at top right.

'You look worried again, Lucy. But as I said, I'll leave you to carry on and here are a couple of web links about those books. I promise not to intrude – you call me back when you're ready. 'Bye, Lucy.'

I swivel away from the desk, switch the kettle on for some coffee and pick up the office phone. I watch in apprehension as my fingers key in the professor's extension.

Line engaged. I'll have to try later. At least there is time to assemble a coherent story. And anyway I ought to check a couple of other web sites relevant to our research project.

Then I should have something to show for my morning's work. But what if Hendrik intervenes? I feel some mental resistance to the idea of trying another workstation, but grit my teeth and make for the departmental library. If Hendrik's presence is exclusive to my machine, this should verify it. Hang on, I tell myself. I'm going there to do some research, not to test for the all-pervasiveness of Hendrik. I shudder at the thought. Soon, I reach the sanctuary of the library and sit at a spare terminal, exploring my desired web sites and then several others, too. I plan to ring Professor Hamilton again at 12.15, just before lunch. But at 11.45 I'm back in my office. What's happening to me? The acute tingling in my fingertips is being assuaged only by contact with the keyboard of my workstation. I pull the mains plug. It kills the machine but otherwise makes no difference.

I pick up the phone. Then pause. If I tell Prof everything, including the physical symptoms, he might send me home. But maybe I *should* go off sick for a while – I could probably get more work done at home, anyway. And so far, Hendrik has not appeared on my home computer. I then realise that more than two hours have passed without seeing Hendrik. I resist the urge to turn my machine back on. With another effort of will, I turn my attention to the phone keypad. Sadie, Prof's Personal Assistant, answers: 'Hi, Lucy! He's out at lunch.'

'OK, I'll call back later – cheers.'

The irritation in my fingers continues while I stand quivering against the edge of my desk. Slowly and deliberately, I take my jacket from the peg behind the door and put it on. I mop my brow with a sleeve and pick up the phone again and leave a message: 'Hi, Sadie. Please tell Prof I'm not feeling too good. I'm off home now for a while. Depending on how I am, I'll ring you tomorrow morning.'

Outside the building, I catch sight of the approaching 19 bus. But my travel-pass isn't in my inside pocket! With alarm, I go through the remaining jacket pockets, then my bag, but to no avail. The bus comes and departs without me. At that moment, a car draws up to the kerb. With relief, I see it's Joe.

'Hello, there! Sadie tells me you're not so well; sorry to hear that. Need a lift?'

'Thanks!'

*****

Chapter 2

I SIT BESIDE Joe in his elderly but very impressive Lotus and we speed off in the direction of the railway station. A train will be an expensive choice without my pass, but quicker. I decide not to tell him the details of my plight, but there's no avoiding mention of the machine.

'How's the new computer doing?' he asks.

'Works fine. Very fast,' I say.

'Good. Mind you, we'll all be getting even newer ones in six months... Here's Victoria Station already.' He looks at his watch 'Not bad, eh?'

'Thanks, Joe.'

'Yep. And before then, Prof wants you researchers to have new home computers hot-mailed to your office workstations and rigged so that you can use them from home. All on the firm, of course.'

'That'll be... very good,' I say, insincerely.

Fortunately, I have enough cash on me to pay the rail fare. The first thing I do on reaching my apartment is to bathe my fingers in warm water. After half an hour, the tingling sensation goes and I have some lunch out of the freezer. Then some black coffee as I doodle on a notepad – drawing a map of events with little boxes and arrows, until I feel everything is as logically connected as I can make it. The central question remains unanswered. Motive? Why is Hendrik doing this? Some kind of sex thing? A power game? I have to know the motive, however complex it might turn out to be. Closely linked to this is Hendrik's identity – is he human, or a cyber-image directed by someone behind the scenes? My experiences run counter to the idea of an actor playing frivolous games. He seems a serious player in a bizarre scheme. What kind of scheme, I've no idea. I have to make some simplifying assumptions. Working backwards, from the scheme angle, my scientific training suggests that it is an elaborate experiment. Who might do this? Of my working colleagues, the professor could set something up with the help of computing experts. His scientific interests are broad enough to encompass the psychology of human-computer interaction. But he seems reasonable and shows compassion. Then there's Joe, the competent technician; quite capable of putting his practical problem solving abilities and computing skills to use. But he's a pragmatist to a degree that would make psychological experimentation an unlikely part of his repertoire. That leaves the computer itself. Where did it go when it was taken away for repair?

I've known Alison since our undergraduate years at Liverpool University. She'd gone on to read medicine while I studied physics. And now, by one of those strange quirks of fate, she's my local GP. I manage to get an appointment at her surgery for later this afternoon.

'The finger irritation baffles me, Lucy,' she says. 'As you've washed your hands, I'll take a couple of swabs from under your fingernails.'

Back home, I take a call at 7.15 pm. It's Alison with some news.

'That was quick,' I say.

'Can I have your permission to dispose of your keyboard, Lucy? Or perhaps take it to the police. Your suspicions are correct. It's contaminated with an alkaloid narcotic that's active through skin absorption.'

This is the confirmation I need. Whoever is perpetrating my problem must be really desperate. Otherwise, why take risks amassing evidence of criminal activity? Things are coming to a head – something is bound to happen soon and I feel scared. Next morning I don't ring Sadie, but I do return to work – a little later than usual, having picked up a replacement keyboard for my machine. I enter my office; hang up my coat and turn around to see Joe standing in the doorway.

'Hello! Feeling better? Oh, yesterday morning I found this outside your door in the corridor,' he says, producing my travel-pass from a pocket of his white lab-coat.

I thank him and he leaves, wheeling a small trolley. I go over to my desk. The workstation is there – except that the keyboard has already been replaced by a different one.

I open my research diary and am about to fire up the computer when a hunch prompts me to do otherwise. Instead, I unwrap my newly purchased keyboard and swap it with the one on my desk, being careful to grip the latter using a sheet of paper, and place it in between the pages of an old magazine in my carrier bag. Now I lock my zipped bag in a filing cabinet before continuing with the day's work.

*****

Chapter 3

AT AFTERNOON BREAK in the staff common-room, Professor Hamilton brings me coffee.

'That was a good set of references and links you unearthed today, Lucy. Very interesting indeed.' He leans a bit closer and continues: 'Glad to see you looking so fit. A couple of days ago you were… well, the least said, the better, eh? The day off has done you a world of good.'

'Thank you,' I say. 'By the way – would it be pushing the boat out if I take a holiday day tomorrow?'

A brief pause. Then: 'No problem at all,' he replies; and in a whisper: 'Don't tell anyone – I won't deduct it from your holiday allocation.'

The remainder of the afternoon passes without incident. Hendrik keeps to his promise and allows me to continue my tasks without interruption. I receive only one e-mail, unsolicited, from a travel company offering amazingly cheap return coach trips out of the City to lots of beauty spots in the UK. I print off a copy including its promotion code and fold it into my coat pocket.

In spite of the advert, I begin my free day with a rail journey – to Reading. I thought I'd take advantage of Hendrik's information of a few days ago. Two of his web links had referred to a forthcoming open-air second-hand book sale near the Town Hall. Great! I arrive early enough to secure two first-editions, one by my favourite science-fiction author. I'm over the moon. The remaining purchases are run-of-the-mill, but they'll appreciate in value, I feel sure. I return home with that very satisfactory 'mission accomplished' feeling. But I open the front door to an unexpected surprise. The place has been ransacked.

The police ask questions, take fingerprints and through the blur of unreality I watch as they do most of the other things done in TV thrillers. Then they leave and a neighbour kindly looks after me. We tidy the place up and I contact Alison, explaining what's happened and that my keyboard would be a different one - if she still doesn't mind examining it. In fact, she insists on calling round. She gives me a mild sedative. I promise to take it when we've finished attending to my apartment.

After we've had something to drink she puts on some gloves to transfer the keyboard from my bag to her own sterile bag. Then I carefully review the list of what had been stolen. It's bad. Fifteen of my rarest books and the hard drives from my desktop workstation and laptop. And I'm still in shock from the mess – 'not very professional', the police had said. I'm particularly aggrieved at the loss of my 'Compendium of Scotia'. It was a well-preserved, one-off, late 18th century piece that was also an heirloom – the very book which started me on the road to collecting.

Alison helps me to continue tidying the place and when she leaves, I carry out some routine tasks - including a cup of strong tea - to distract myself from the intrusion and loss. Fortunately, I'd adopted the habit of backing up my hard drives and I'm relieved to find the copied files safe and sound in the bedroom. I transfer the relevant contents onto a spare laptop. The files are a couple of weeks out of date, but that doesn't matter for my immediate purpose. Ironically, I end up examining a series of images of interest that I'd scanned from my book collection several months ago. In particular, pages 366 and 367 of the stolen Compendium. I remember when my grandfather, its previous owner, had sat me on his knee when I was twelve years old and said that I should find these pages of interest, as they concerned our family. But I've never been a historian in the true sense or had much interest in family tree stuff. And I could hardly read the script. So last year, when eventually I bought a scanner, I digitised several pages with a view to grappling with their contents at a later date. *Thank goodness I did!* This is now the only link I have with my grandfather, Alex MacKinnon Dow.

And I feel that *now* is the time to deal with it! Using an art package to enhance the images on my computer screen, the text becomes more readable... I learn that Grandfather Dow's line of the family wanted to join the Jacobite cause and fight under the banner of Clan Buchanan at the 1746 battle of Culloden near Inverness. As I read on, I forget my anxieties and become riveted to the fragment of history unwinding before me.

Apparently, the Clan Buchanan had a problem. Its territories were situated along the eastern side of Loch Lomond, not far from the Campbells who were opposed to the Jacobites. So rather than fight openly, the Buchanans ostensibly backed off, and left the Dows with a nod and a wink to make up their own minds.

The outcome at Culloden had been anticipated by a fair proportion of participants on the Highland side. A lack of sufficient support from English Catholics during the Scots' march towards London, followed by their about-turn at Derby and their return to Scotland, were indeed frustrating developments. Added to these were the climate of disillusionment, fear of treachery and the possibility of defeat. A perfect storm was brewing, which prompted a group of leaders to hold a secret meeting. According to the book, much of the wealth the Jacobite army carried was in the safekeeping of a trusted few, including Robert Alexander Dow, my grandfather's ancestor. He became party to a scheme to bury four fifths of the entire reserve in a location known only to five men.

Unfortunately, all five were killed in the ensuing rout at Culloden. It seemed the cache would never be found. But the book said that before the battle, Robert Alexander's son, Fergus, was told a riddle by his father. It was a coded mixture of Scots dialect and Gaelic, in case he should be captured by the English. Sure enough, Fergus was taken prisoner. But during a violent thunderstorm he stole a horse and escaped, with help from a camp follower - a girl whom he later married, and they reared a family in Dumfries. That was my grandfather's birthplace. Already I'm into the last paragraph of page 367 with no further mention of the coded message. Could it be 'overleaf' on page 368? I click on the image and enlarge it... The answer? No, because the last sentence includes a stipulation that the final part of the message would be passed on only by word of mouth.

Disappointing - but possibly a blessing in disguise, making it hard work for would-be prospectors of Jacobite gold. I'm already aware of the recent reported find of musket balls and coins at Sandaig on the shores of Loch nan Uamh. But according to the missing book, my ancestor's hoard is thought to be further south, hidden somewhere near Dumfries in the Scottish Borders.

In my profession, I'm used to looking for patterns in events and data, but now I'm confused. How does all this connect, if at all, with the happenings of the last few days? It's midnight. I switch off my computer, take Alison's pill and climb into bed for a few hours of fitful sleep.

*****

Chapter 4

NEXT DAY, IN spite of the professor's understanding and sympathy following my recent experience, I say nothing about the missing Compendium. And back at my office desk, I run the gauntlet of using my workstation. The rest of the morning goes smoothly. Hendrik is conspicuous by his absence. All day, I hear nothing from him. But I make sure that if he's monitoring my machine usage, my work schedule appears perfectly normal. In other words, research project from start to finish. I have the satisfaction of denying him any opportunity to gloat over my misfortunes. I'm ready to leave when the telephone rings at my elbow. It's Alison.

'I'm sorry to ring you at work. Are you free at 7 o'clock this evening? I think you should come over here.'

Seated on Alison's sofa, I look around her lounge for the keyboard. No sign of it.

'If I've guessed correctly, what you're looking for isn't here,' my host says.

'Oh?'

'It's in a laboratory at the Institute of Tropical Medicine. I delivered it this morning. The results of their tests were e-mailed to me at 3.45 this afternoon. Bad news, I'm afraid. How many people have you been in physical contact with since you touched it?'

'None. And I didn't touch it. Not directly, that is.' I explain about the paper and magazine wrapping I used.

'Good. But I've arranged for you to have tests tomorrow morning at the Intstitute – Dr. Moran, 10.15.'

'Please, Alison. What's this all about?'

'I'm sorry to have to give you a second shock so soon. Would you like some tea before we discuss it?'

'No, thank you. Please tell me straight.'

'Well, your bag which contained the keyboard must also be disposed of. If you wish, I'll deal with it. The point is - whoever tampered with the keyboard this time wanted you out of the way – permanently! Fortunately though, the bacillus only survives a couple of hours at most outside the human body. And if no symptoms develop within the next four days, you're in the clear. And if tomorrow's blood test is negative, you should be okay.'

'Then they got what they came for…'

'How do you mean, Lucy?'

She knows about my stolen books, but not the details.

'Some of my missing books might be quite valuable,' I say.

'You think the incidents are linked?'

'Don't know – just a guess.'

'I think you should talk to the police,' Alison said. 'No doubt they'll be calling on you again, and I'll have to report my findings on both of your keyboards.'

Next morning, I ring in to work to let them know of my hospital visit and that I should remain at home until the result was known. At 4.30pm Alison rings with the all-clear.

She adds: 'And I'm writing a sick note to give you a week's rest after all this!'

In a state of joyous relief, I begin to prepare myself some tea when the doorbell rings. I look up into a moon-like face with incisive steel grey eyes:

'Inspector Gordon Richards, Thames Valley Police,' he announces, holding his card aloft. He looks well-built, in his mid forties at a guess, and clad in a trench coat of the kind beloved by his profession. 'Good evening... Miss Doe?'

'Dow.' I correct him.

He squeezes past me into the lounge, and then opens a blue folder. By the time he's finished questioning me, it's past 9 o'clock.

'Thanks for your help,' he says. 'Will you be around here for the next few days?'

'Well, I might…' A plan is forming in my mind. The events of the last few days have exhausted me. I need that break: 'I might to go to Scotland.' The words seem to come of their own accord.

The Inspector raises an eyebrow. 'When, and for how long?' he asks.

Unsure, banking on the professor's acceptance of my note and thinking on my feet, I reply: 'From the day after tomorrow, for three or four days.'

'Then please keep me informed of your whereabouts and accommodation address.' On the way out he pauses and gives me the first smile of the evening. 'You can telephone me using the number on your copy of the statement form, Miss - er - Dow.'

Back in my study, I retrieve my coach travel leaflet. The price of the tickets is tempting. If the stolen Compendium is already being put to use, it seems logical to chase it by the most convenient means. If the thief had planned for my possible survival of the keyboard attack, would he expect me to follow him to Scotland? And would he assume I'd use the coach service shown in the screen-ad? Hendrik knows of my penchant for bargains, which makes me even more suspicious about the unsolicited travel e-mail at my workplace. He also knows that I'd be determined to recover my book. And that to have any hope at all, I'd have to act quickly. Perhaps he has access to further information? Yes, and he would possibly have the coaches watched at the nearest stop to where he thought the hoard's burial place might be. But according to the leaflet, that would have to be either Dungowrie or Moffat, with Dungowrie the strongest bet. If I travel alone, I risk stepping off the coach into some sort of trap. But there's no companion I can find at such short notice. My hands shake as I pour myself another cup of tea. Perhaps the trauma of the theft and its aftermath is making me paranoid. As if to underline this, I fantasise about going in disguise!

The moustache tickles more than I expect, and I have to blow my nose several times - I dare not sneeze, as my sneezes sound so very feminine. Otherwise, the journey is refreshingly scenic. At Dungowrie, a fellow passenger kindly assists me off the coach.

'Thank you,' I whisper, smiling in appreciation as she hands me my walking stick.

I hope that my slight limp will mask any inconsistencies between the disguise and my pelvic configuration, as I make for the bus-station's gents toilets. It's a hot day and the urinals reek. I move hastily to a closet. On emerging, I see a shadowy figure out of the corner of my eye. It's him. He steps off the wet stone platform and nearly collides with me.

'Sorry, mate!' he says.

Avoiding eye contact, I grunt as deeply as I can and wave dismissively with my free hand. With my shoulder bag hoisted I exit the building, remembering to limp and use my walking stick. I dare not hurry and grit my teeth as he overtakes me and makes for a vacant seat near one of the bus stages. I take a paper handkerchief to my nose, using it as a mask as I watch him. He glances about the bus station whilst idly turning the pages of his book. But even at 20 yards I can see it was not his book – but my book! As my hand drops from my face, I feel the air on my upper lip. I look down to see the moustache twitching in the breeze on the concrete flagstones. I happen to be standing next to a group of half a dozen schoolchildren. Before I can bend down, one of them reaches it before me.

'Here's yer wee hairy thing!' he says, waving the object aloft like a prize. To the accompaniment of his colleagues' ribald laughter, he ceremoniously hands it to me.

'Thanks!' I murmur, in my normal voice. Then I see Hendrik look in my direction and rise from his seat. 'Yes, I'm most grateful,' I continue, 'I'll need this moustache for the film rehearsal tonight. I'm just an extra, but you see that guy walking towards us? Recognise him? He's a really famous TV star!'

'Yeah?' The leader of the group frowns uncertainly. 'Who is he?'

'Surely, you must know! Go and find out, then!' I say with heartfelt urgency. 'You'd all better get his autograph while you can.'

Not wishing to appear ignorant or indecisive, the ringleader turns to the group. 'Come on!' he bellows. As one, they charge and surround Hendrik, fumbling for notebooks or scraps of paper.

Meanwhile, one of the local buses begins revving its engine. I jump aboard.

'Where to?' asks the driver.

Every second seems an age as I try to put my brain into gear. 'Five stops,' I say.

'The Classic Cinema?'

'Yes.'

'That's one pound, sir - er, madam.'

I scrabble among the tissues in my coat pocket. Through the window, beyond the driver, Hendrik has freed himself from the mob. At his vulture-like sequence of darting glances, I freeze. My searching hand tightens involuntarily to a clenched fist. Then I feel an object pressing into my knuckles. I pull the pound coin from my pocket and at last the doors hiss shut behind me. As we lurch towards the main road, I collapse into a seat on the side of the bus away from

Hendrik. We are on our way and for the moment I'm safe. But then the bus swings sharp left onto the main road and pulls into a bus stop. I'm once more a visible target. As the bus moves off he sees me, jumps out of his car, and is running towards the bus. But then the bus picks up speed. Even so, it's only a matter of moments before he returns to his car and catches up. I reason that as long as I remain on the bus, I should be all right. Even if he's armed, he wouldn't dare to board the bus and threaten me. He would still be hanging on to my book – I could accuse him of stealing it and cause a commotion. But he would still want me out of the way before recovering the hoard; so he would tail me from a distance, awaiting his opportunity. On the other hand, as long as he has the book, I can't afford to lose him.

Two stops further on, I see Hendrik at the wheel of his car, following 100 yards behind. He's in a four-by-four with knobbly tyres, stopping as the bus stops.

I feel panic welling up inside me as my journey nears its end. 'Three more stops, please,' I say to the driver.

'That'll be another sixty pence, please.'

As I hand it over, the car overtakes us. I realise he knows that I wouldn't want him out of my sight. On impulse, I grab a pencil from my bag and take down the registration number of the car. Probably hired, anyway. Just before I close my bag, my mobile phone rings.

It's Inspector Richards.

'Hello, Inspector! I'm on a bus in Dungowrie - what number's this bus?' I ask the driver.

'Huh? It was 16 when I set off, I don't think it's changed!'

'Number 16,' I relay to the Inspector. Then aside to the driver: 'Are we going towards town or away?'

He rolls his eyes to the roof of his cabin. I'm worried in case his vehicle should hit something.

'See that notice? Don't distract the driver while the bus is in motion. We're going into town - now go and sit down, please.'

I gabble a description of current events into my phone, including the car's registration number.'

'That's fine.' Inspector Richards intones his phlegmatic reply as if it's a prelude to an afternoon nap. 'I'll arrange for somebody to investigate your problem as soon as I can. Goodbye, Miss Dow.'

I lose count of the stops, but needn't worry. The driver glances in my direction.

'Your's is the next stop,' he says nonchalantly.

Everyone is so laid back, I thought. My heart is racing as I deliberate about staying on longer - perhaps to the terminus. But I've run out of small change. I grit my teeth and offer up a £20 note.

'You're winding me up, my dear, aren't ye?' he says, as he pulls into the bus stop and waves me on my way. The car also stops, about 50 yards up the road. A passenger brushes past me and steps off the bus. I follow her through the door, stuffing the note into my pocket. Then I catch up with the passenger.

'Excuse me, can you please tell me the way to the police station?' I ask. The sound of the bus moving off forces me to repeat the question.

'Aye. We passed it half a mile back,' she says, 'Get the 16 or 22 bus on the other side of the road.'

Then a thought flashes through my mind. 'Is there a railway station near here?'

She looks at me quizzically, her wrinkled brow furrowing under her headscarf.

'Ye'll need tae go the other way. Get off at Lockerbie. Here's yer bus the noo!'

'Thanks!' I shout, crossing the road. I flag down a number 22 at the bus stop.

'Aye?' the driver asks..

'Railway station, please.'

'Lockerbie? Two pounds forty.'

The driver frowns at my £20 note and glances at my walking stick. 'Nae less? Och! Sit ye doon,' he mutters, nodding towards a vacant seat.

'Sorry!' I whisper.

His response is to thrust the vehicle into gear and nearly send me flying down the aisle. We lurch past Hendrik's parked car, which promptly starts off again. He follows the bus all the way to Lockerbie. The traffic density increases and within five minutes I see a sign for the railway station. I'd have to get off at the next stop. Without leaving my seat I press the bell and then mingle with the several passengers making for the exit. When I get off, Hendrik has moved on again to park about 100 yards ahead, just the other side of a zebra crossing, on the start of the yellow lines. A policeman is walking towards his car. I break cover and make for the crossing. The policeman goes to the front of Hendrik's car, his arm raised. Hendrik opens the door of his car. I panic and veer across the street.

'Excuse me, sir. Is this your vehicle?' I hear the policeman ask.

At the central bollards, I couldn't resist looking back. I saw Hendrik hesitate; he glances in my direction, then at the policeman. I too hesitate. Should I rush over to the policeman and tell him? Or should I carry on towards the railway station? I've had enough. I want to quit. Let Hendrik dig for treasure if he wants. It's not the end of the world if I fail to regain possession of my book - or any part of the treasure that might be mine by right. I believe he would still try to follow me, though. Even if he knows that the police would be onto him - I'm convinced he's mad enough.

However, I pull myself together and wheel around ready to face him.

The road is clear and I run towards the policeman.

'Officer!' I shout. 'This man has something of mine - a rare book…'

'Indeed? Are ye suggesting there has been an offence, Miss?' The policeman - actually a young constable - reaches for his smart phone. 'Are you saying it was stolen?'

'Borrowed,' Hendrik interrupts. 'The lady loaned it me a few days ago. She's under some strain, as you can see. I'm sure we can settle the matter without any fuss, can't we, my dear?' My skin crawls at his syrupy words.

'Officer, I happen to know that this man is wanted for questioning by Inspector Richards of Thames Valley Police, not only for this theft…'

Hendrik laughs disdainfully. 'She really is quite ill, you know,' he says with theatrical gravity.

'…but attempted murder.' My disclosure evokes a raised eyebrow from the constable but has little effect on Hendrik.

'I do apologise for parking here and I'd better move the car immediately. But I'll be quite happy to answer any further questions you may have, Constable.'

'Before ye move on, sir, perhaps you could ease the situation by returning the lady's book?'

The faintest shadow crosses Hendrik's face. 'Of course, sir. It's in the back - I'll get it.' He opens the rear door and rummages around for several seconds in the boot and then hands me the book.

'Thank you,' I say.

'My pleasure - thank *you* for the loan of it.'

I turn to the policeman: 'And Constable, here is the telephone extension of Inspector Richards for you to verify what I said before.' I hand him a torn scrap of paper.

'Thank you, Miss. I'll look into the matter.'

He doesn't believe me! I realise.

'I hope you at least have the car number!' I say, knowing I'm displeasing him by telling him his job.

'You'd better cross now, Miss,' he suggests, 'while the traffic is clear.'

With the book under my arm, I do exactly that. I reach the other side of the road to see the reflection of myself in the window of a department store. The shadow on my upper lip! Throughout the tension of the confrontation I'd forgotten that the moustache was back in place. I'm convinced that this and the rest of my theatrical attire have conspired with my female voice to reduce my credibility to zero. I hurry to the railway station, removing the offending lip décor as I go.

*****

Chapter 5

NOTING THE DISPLAYED train times, I cross the concourse and buy a ticket for the next train out. Inverness, and why not? I'd like to visit Culloden. I'm sure Hendrik believes that now I have the book, I'll be hurrying back to London. But once he's satisfied the policeman, he has a choice. I guess there's a good chance he now has all of the information he can get from the book, and having returned it he'll let me go. Depending on how much info' he's gathered and interpreted, he might even get digging before dark. Even though the policeman hadn't believed my accusation, Hendrik might feel close to being a prime suspect. Now, hopefully, he'll not stalk or threaten me. Even so, I choose a rear-facing seat and search the platform, but there's no sign of him. The train begins to pull out and I sit back to fondly caress my book. There are only three other passengers in my carriage, and they aren't looking in my direction. I remove my coat and rearranged my hair, so that my appearance is almost back to normal. Again, I lift the leather bound volume. It's wonderful to savour the smell of the pages as I turn them. Then suddenly, I curse Hendrik aloud, to the alarm of the nearest person a few seats away. As many as eight pages - including the vital ones, of course - have been torn out. So that's what he was doing in the back of his car!

The bed and breakfast I find at Inverness is homely and very pleasant, with a fine view of the mountains from my bedroom window – just a hint of morning haze which I know would soon disperse. Unfortunately, Hendrik is never far from my thoughts. By now he could possibly be gloating over his treasure trove, not that I believe he'd be declaring it to the authorities. I try speculating where the dig is located. Even an hour's drive in any direction would take in a wide area. Without precise data, simple geometry would suggest a search area covering several thousand square miles.

But Hendrik is no longer my problem – at least for the time being. I cross the bedroom and turn on the television for the remainder of the morning news. The sports items give way to local reports. I pick up my leather bound book to look again at the damage. But my attention is brought back to the screen.

The reporter's flame-red hair catches the wind as she holds out her mike to a farmer standing by his Land Rover.

'…and what did you see next?' she asks.

'This guy's Shogun moved up the hillside and went behind some bushes. Then I heard a crunching sound and silence. I thought he'd broken down.'

'So you went to investigate?'

'Sure. I took my car up to see if I could help.'

The picture panned towards the farmer's Land Rover showing a front bumper bar equipped with a winch.

'And when you got there…?'

'There was just silence and this big hole in the ground. There was nothing I could do, so I called 999. We had the police, ambulance and fire brigade here, and eventually the vehicle was pulled clear.'

While he speaks, the next pictures show the gaping hole. Next to it is a crumpled four-by-four. The camera pans across the wreckage, revealing the buckled front registration plate. I can just about read it. It's Hendrik's!

The reporter continues: 'The driver had to be cut out of the wreckage, but he was unfortunately dead on arrival at hospital.'

The scene switched to an interview with an official looking balding man in his late 50s wearing a well tailored suit. The interviewee was expressing concern that there may be other concealed mine-shafts in the area and that too many off-roaders were ignoring the warning notices.

'And what will become of the cache of gold coins unearthed by the vehicle on its way down?' the reporter asks.

'There were small but potentially dangerous boxes of gunpowder – black powder of the type used in 18th century firearms – and many of the coins were caked with the powder.'

'So the cache was booby-trapped?'

'Aye. Anyone searching with a lighted torch of the period would have come to sticky end. The whole thing would have become a shrapnel grenade. But as you can see, the army has the area cordoned off and they expect to recover all of the coins by the end of the week.'

'Are there other finds like this likely in these hills?'

'We think not. The documentary evidence recovered from the victim's car has been examined by experts. It looks like this was the only hoard of its kind and that there's certainly no justification in digging up the countryside in the hope of finding any more.'

'Did the documentation reveal anything about ownership - whose money it is?

'Yes. I understand that technically it's treasure trove. But the documents reveal certain families by name which could benefit from the discovery.'

'Does that include the victim's family?'

'A computer search has already been carried out. And the answer is no, I'm afraid not.'

'Thank you, Mr. MacEwan. And now, back to the studio. Jessie Craig from Watchman Hill, near Elvanfoot.'

Three days later I arrive back at my apartment in London. I restore my book to its rightful place on the shelf in my bedroom. Then I begin composing a letter to Inspector

Richards, in the hope that he'll help me recover the missing pages and advise me on procedures for checking my eligibility for a claim on the find. I post the letter in the morning on my way to work.

At my desk, the computer workstation now comes up with the customary university home page, which I skip in readiness to begin my first set of tasks. Everything goes well until the morning coffee break, when suddenly my computer bleeps. Incoming e-mail? I look up. It's Hendrik's face again on the screen!

'Hello, Lucy. Please don't turn off your machine…'

'Stuff you!' I cry, yanking the plug out of the wall-socket. I nearly fall flat on my face as I jump up and trip over the chair castors. My coffee mug goes flying. I dash along the corridor and up the flight of stairs to the professor's room. My heart is pounding and I gasp for breath as I hammer on his door.

'Good heavens, Lucy!' says Sadie, 'What's the matter?'

'Where's the professor?' I ask.

'He won't be back until after lunch – try after 2 o'clock.'

Reluctantly, I return to my workstation and sit thinking for several minutes. Why is Hendrik still active? Was he really driving that 4x4? It must have been him. I feel my right foot squish on the carpet pile. My mug had rolled under the desk. Just then, Janet the cleaner appears as if from nowhere.

'Oh dear!' she says. 'Let me sort out that mess for you!'

She retrieves the mug, rinses it and pours me some fresh coffee. I thank her; then, as she leaves, I decide to do the unthinkable. Firing up the workstation, I wait for Hendrik to appear again. And he does.

'Hello Lucy. Please don't turn off your machine…' It's an exact re-run. Then a short pause is followed by a passage of

music. A sombre funeral march. *'This particular message,'* Hendrik's voice continues, *'signifies that I am no longer alive.'*

*****

Chapter 6

I FEEL MY mouth go dry and a shiver runs down my spine.
'However, Lucy, there is something I must tell you.'

'What now?' I mutter. The talking head image in the top right quadrant of the screen continues: *'There is no time to waste. Put on your headphones and when you're ready, press the escape key.'*

Where is my headset? It's in the middle drawer of my desk – I take it out and hastily jam the phones over my ears. What key is it? Escape. Immediately, the talking head resumes: *'Go back to Scotland. Make for Moffat and see Sheriff Carnegie. He's a former member of the Treasure Trove Unit and will make sure you recover what is due to you. He – or one of his colleagues – will eventually take custody of my documents, and also your missing pages. Don't tell anyone – just go. Now. And I'm sorry for all the trouble I've...'* The screen goes blank and there's a loud click in my headset. Then silence. Why the apology? I wonder. This seems out of character, considering all that has happened. For several minutes I ponder his last request. Then I make up my mind.

Obediently, I collect my bag and put on my coat.

'I'm not feeling too well again, Sadie,' I say.

'Hope you feel better soon, Lucy. You do look a bit pale. I'm sure the professor won't mind if you look after yourself for a couple of days.'

I head back to my office to collect a couple of research papers to read on my journey. As I descend the stairs toward the corridor, I hear the sound of a distant trolley being wheeled away. I grab some more papers out of my filing cabinet and glance at my desk to make sure I have everything I need. It's then that I notice the computer has gone! Even the mouse and keyboard. There was a scrawled note: *On the network, I detected a fault on your machine – it should be back by tomorrow morning. Joe.*

Funnily enough, when I arrive home, I'm unwell. I feel terrible. So bad that I ring Alison, hoping I'll catch her before she leaves her surgery. The long and short of it is, within three hours I'm back at the hospital sweating profusely and hallucinating. A few days later, while I recuperate on the ward, the consultant tells me he had diagnosed the very tropical disease from which I had escaped before, and that without my precautionary vaccination on the previous visit, I would not have survived.

'Like last time, I've asked your GP and my staff to keep the nature of this infection quiet, so as not to hinder investigations,' he says.

As I leave the hospital, I have to accept postponement of my journey to Moffat. As I make my way to the bus stop, a familiar car draws up at the kerbside. It's Joe. A wave of apprehension passes through me. Was it the keyboard again? And is Joe involved? This time I had no proof of either possibility. But maybe the infection was from another source. The book? Then I remember, Hendrik was wearing driving gloves when he returned it to me. Tears filled my eyes at the thought of having to dispose of my book. Then I recall that the bacillus has a short lifetime outside a patient. And Joe's engaging manner puts me at ease.

'Hi there!' he says, cheerily. 'I only heard yesterday about you being in hospital. I called to ask about visiting, but they told me you were already discharged and on your way out. I thought I'd collect you and take you all the way home, if that's OK.'

I thank him. 'That's very kind of you, Joe. It's better than the crowded train,' I say as we speed off.

Joe looks again in my direction. 'You must have been through a lot,' he said. 'It can't be much fun going down with a weird tropical disease. It makes you wonder who you're sitting next to on flights abroad – I bet it's all this air travel…'

'Who told you it was a tropical disease?' I immediately regret my outburst – and with it, the lost opportunity to play dumb.

'Our duty receptionist,' he says, his eyes on the driving mirror.

He is lying, I feel sure.

'We turn left here, Joe,' I remind him. But he speeds past the end of my road and on into open countryside.

'It's OK, Lucy – I've realised there's something urgent I have to attend to.'

'It's not OK, Joe. Please turn back or let me out of the car now.' We continue to accelerate, and as we round the next bend on two wheels the vehicle swerves into another lane, just missing an oncoming wagon. Then a building comes into view behind some trees. Against the grey sky I recognise the silhouette on Briar's Hill. I've seen the disused barn on Farmer Berry's land from this angle before and dread fills the pit of my stomach as we bounce along the overgrown track towards it. I try the car door but draw back in alarm as the hedge scrapes against the bodywork.

Then suddenly there is a loud bang and my feet lift off the floor. Joe's low-slung sports car was designed for the flat tarmac, not for off-roading over hidden boulders. The passenger door bursts open and the next instant I'm on the ground in long grass. The hedge looms above me and I roll to try to get up. I raise myself onto my knees but see no sign of the car. Even though the other side of the track is only a few yards away, it seems a long and painful crawl. Then I see that the car has spun off the road and is lying on its side at the bottom of an embankment.

Without thinking, I half crawl and half slither down the slope to Joe's aid, trying to avoid the crystalline fragments of broken glass. Then my fear wells up again. Forcefully, I drag myself across the crackling stubble at the edge of the field and peer through the gaping hole where the windscreen had been. The car is resting on its driver's side. Joe is in there, moving slowly. He gasps – either with pain or fear – I can't tell. He's still in the driver's seat, his weight on his right arm, which is jammed between him and the driver's door. Slowly, very slowly, he works his arm free. It's bleeding and small shards of glass are embedded in the sleeve. At first, I assumed the glass was from the vehicle – but some pieces look partly cylindrical or tubular. I couldn't see his jacket pocket very well, but it might have been torn.

Then he looks at me. His mouth works, but nothing comes. Then, his face deathly pale, he rasps: 'Sorry, Lucy.'

'It was an accident,' I shout. 'Let's get you out of here!'

His eyes seem to look through me before he lowers them again in the direction of his sleeve. 'Meant for you...' are his last words. He slumps, then spasms slightly, and lays still.

When the paramedics arrive, it's dark. That's all I can remember, until I look up from my hospital bed into the languid eyes of Inspector Richards. During his fourth questioning attempt of the day (the hospital staff are very good to me) I learn from him that the broken ampoule in Joe's pocket had contained a nerve toxin. It was again a plant alkaloid, possibly taken from another laboratory where he had been employed as a technician, before his job with the professor

From then on, I recover quickly. And so it is that I find myself being discharged from hospital twice within the same week. I suppose they needed the beds. Anyway, as soon as I arrive home, the phone rings.

'I'd like to call and deliver a package to you,' the Inspector says.

I invite him round for that evening and over some buttered scones and tea, he explains the happenings in more detail.

'The sheriff up at Moffat…' the Inspector pauses to hold up a scone, examining it thoughtfully. He scratches at the corner of his eye with his little finger as he continues: 'Carnegie, that's him – he sent me some things for you, by special delivery.'

'I was on my way to see him before taking ill,' I say.

'There's probably no urgency now - open your package.'

With his free hand he passes me a packet. It had been marked 'IN CONFIDENCE' but opened and re-sealed with a label: 'SECURITY CHECKED'. His heavy jaw slowly works the scone while I tear open the envelope.

He startles me with a burp and then apologises, adding: 'Nice cooking, Miss Dow.' His Adam's apple bobs in confirmation of my scone's demise and he begins to sip his tea rather noisily. 'Er… in there you'll see a few book pages,' he says. 'And a covering letter. Its contents are private, but we had to read it… in the line of duty, you understand.'

Even so, I feel invaded. And I pretend not to notice his pale beady eyes studying my face. The letter is a word processor printout, written in Hendrik's style but with a strange signature that I don't recognise. Running along the fold across the middle is a rust-like brownish stain that might be dried blood.

'Please go ahead and read it,' says the Inspector.

For some reason my hands start shaking. I grit my teeth and obey.

Dear Lucy,

If you are reading this it is too late – for me, at least. We have never met, properly, face to face. I wish we had - how I wish we had! When I first saw your camera image I knew I wanted to meet you. The mission to find the money wasn't my idea, originally. It started in Glasgow, where I am – was – a journalist. I received a telephone call from one of your associates, whom I must call X. We'd met a long time ago at a tennis club and kept loosely in touch ever since. Anyway, back in March last year, X began asking me questions about the Culloden mystery. I didn't know anything special, but it sounded interesting. X was very keen on the idea of finding the Culloden gold. I was tempted, and an exclusive story could be my big break to get into television.

I spent most of the summer combing the web for information. But X was right - the path led to you as the strongest lead, being a direct descendent who was also on the internet. So now you know why I hadn't come to you directly. I had already started on the collaborative venture with X and I decided to find out as much as possible about you before making contact. That wasn't difficult – the university web pages told me a lot about your academic background and your own page described your hobbies in some detail.

At this point the ink becomes illegible. Below the stain, it continues:

...several times. But each time I was scared I would frighten you off. I wanted you desperately to come with me to the dig. But things had already taken a sinister turn and I knew we were being watched. My so-called friend turned out to be not so friendly once I wanted you in on the deal. X told me that if I didn't drop you, it would be the worse for my career. I said I didn't care – I wanted you to have your

rightful share, all of it. At this point, X claimed to have underground connections and said that if I didn't 'play ball' and help find the gold, something nasty would be arranged for both of us. Not playing ball included any attempt to get in touch with you. So that's why you had to come to Scotland under your own volition. And it's also why I cannot divulge the identity of this collaborator, even now. The police will have to find out under their own steam. Whatever has happened to me to bring about this situation, remember – I love you, Lucy. If the treasure is found, claim your part of it. Meanwhile, watch your back.

All my love – Lars Petersen.

*****

Chapter 7

'IS – WAS – LARS his name?' I ask the Inspector through tear-filled eyes.

'Yes, Lucy. That was his real name.' This is the first time the Inspector calls me by my Christian name.

'He was a… rather different person than I expected.' I immediately regret the feebleness of my understatement and still feel embarrassment in the presence of Inspector Richards. But new feelings are growing inside me – simultaneous feelings of love and loss. Thoughts of what might have been. My eyes stray to a vase of red roses on the sideboard and rest there. Alison had brought them on my return from the hospital. I pull myself back to the harshness of the real world.

'Who's the colleague Hendrik – I mean Lars – calls X?' I asked. 'Was it Joe?'

'That would wrap it up, wouldn't it?' the Inspector says. 'But it is only fair to warn you that I think this case is far from closed.'

'How do you mean?'

Richards smiles grimly. 'Call it professional intuition, if you like. Joe was clearly involved, but he had the hallmarks of an amateur. For instance, look how he carried around in his jacket pocket that unprotected thin glass ampoule containing one of the most deadly toxins known to humanity. All the more surprising for a technician trained in safety procedures. No, our friend Joe was quite a small fish, which means I'm still looking for someone.'

'Do you have a suspect in mind,' I ask.

'Yes.'

'Am I allowed to ask who?'

'You have to understand, Lucy,' he says, 'it's a very delicate situation. For my investigation to get anywhere, it's essential that your behaviour remains normal. You must act as if you had never read Hendrik's letter – and make sure you always refer to him as Hendrik. Also, and this is crucial, behave as if you suspect nobody in particular. Otherwise you could be in very real danger. That's why I cannot disclose to you the identity of my prime suspect. Besides, as yet I have no hard evidence.'

'What about the keyboards? And the computer being taken away for repair? I asked.

'I can only repeat, I have no proof. There were no fingerprints except yours on the first keyboard, and none, again apart from yours, on the second. The computer itself had Joe's prints all over it. But you would expect that. On-site equipment maintenance was part of his job. The ampoule fragments in Joe's pocket required careful handling, but there were no prints, other than Joe's.'

I feel like a spare part, thoroughly frustrated at the prospect of being a mere spectator. 'I could help you trace Joe's contacts,' I suggest. 'I'm well placed to do some background work from inside the university.'

'Yes, too obviously, I'm afraid. I'd prefer it if you left things to me, Lucy. And that extends to contacting Joe's parents or other family members. They are very distraught, but I've had them briefed not to discuss the case with anyone.'

'It's going to be very difficult for me back at work. Who is left on the suspect list apart from the professor? How will I put up with seeing him almost every day, the hours passing by while he might be getting away with it, and I'm just sitting around like a lemon?'

'What did I say about behaving as if you suspect nobody? Sure, it's not going to be easy, but to be effective, your practice begins now.'

I apologise. Then: 'I'd be quite happy,' I suggest, 'for your people to wire me up while you use listening devices.'

'I'm not prepared to risk it. As I said, just leave everything to us. Don't worry; they won't get away with it. But we have to be patient.'

Don't worry! I'm prompted to ask him about his use of the word 'they', but resist the temptation.

He cocks his head back slightly, jutting his jaw and fixing me with his beady stare. 'There is one thing you can do for us, Lucy.'

'Yes, Inspector?' I ask eagerly.

'If anyone - and I mean *anyone* - should ask you about suspects, you can say you've been told by me that so far there are none.'

'OK.' At least I might be planting some information – or mis-information.

He gets up. 'Thank you again for your hospitality and co-operation, Miss Dow. Look after yourself.'

I close the door behind him and shiver involuntarily.

A week later I go round to Alison's surgery to thank her for the flowers and to sign me off sick leave.

'Hello soldier,' she says.

I admit to feeling as if I've been through some kind of major campaign. 'Thank goodness it's finished with,' I say.

'I saw the TV reports. The local one described how your kidnapper came to grief on Briar's Hill. Looks like he was the keyboard culprit. With him and Hendrik out of it, you can get back to normal again. If you feel you need a counsellor, I can put you in touch with one.'

'No thanks – I'll be fine. I'm just glad it's all over!' I say, hoping to close the subject.

'All right. If you change your mind, just let me know. Anyway, I'm glad to hear you've had your book returned.'

How does she know that? I wonder. Alison must have read my face.

'The Inspector in his recent rounds of questioning mentioned there were a few torn pages,' she says. 'More to the point, though, you are in one piece and it's so wonderful to see you again.' She gives me an affectionate hug and adds: 'If you're quite sure, there'll be no problem signing you back to work.'

When I arrive at Sadie's office to hand in my doctor's note, she puts an arm around my shoulder and insists on strong coffee for both of us.

'And listen!' she says, 'We've arranged for you to have another office. Just two doors next to the Professor. And for the next few weeks, we'll make sure you take things easy. If there's anything you need, please ask us.'

Without saying so, I feel some disappointment. I've grown to like my previous office. It overlooked the city, and the winding river beyond. My new room has a south-easterly prospect, which means I'll miss the lurid winter sunsets.

*****

Chapter 8

THE FOLLOWING MORNING, I'm about to re-arrange my new office when the telephone rings. It's the Professor.

'Good morning, Lucy! Could you please come into my office?'

'Good morning. Yes, Professor!'

This seems a bit strange - he being only two doors away.

After I enter, he gestures me to close the door. Then I understand the reason.

In the professor's office, Sadie looks so relaxed in the leather armchair. But her weapon hand never wavers.

The Professor sits on an upright wooden chair near the window, an occasional twitch contorting his scowling face.

'Sadie! You think you can get away with this?' he snarls.

'Either way, your career is over, Professor Hamilton,' Sadie replies. 'Lucy here, on the other hand, will be remembered as a clever but perhaps rather naive professional. That's why I owe her an explanation for all this. You're welcome to listen and correct any fine details, Professor.'

'I doubt if it will be worth the effort,' he sneers.

'As you wish.' Sadie turns to me. 'By the end of last year,' she continued, 'Prof's research income had dried up completely. And that was the excuse the Vice-Chancellor and his minions had been waiting for. To delegate – or rather, to off-load – a very substantial amount of administration. It wasn't long before dear Prof here was bored out of his mind with it all. He felt persecuted and manipulated by the university hierarchy. He was stressed out and went for treatment on several occasions. Sit down, Professor! While I'm addressing Lucy, my peripheral vision has no problem detecting movement. Where was I? Yes. Then, all at once, he received some good news – didn't you, Prof? In February this year he landed a research grant, most of which eventually became the salary for your post, Lucy.'

'He's been doing a lot of research since I came,' I say.

'Sure. Not only that, he began by pushing back the tide of rubbish that had overwhelmed him and resolved that it would never happen again.' Sadie turns towards the Professor. 'But his new-found energies and aspirations took a rather bizarre turn, didn't they?'

'Speak for yourself!' the Professor's chair creaked as he leaned back defiantly.

'Shut up! I won't warn you again. Well, Lucy, he had it in for the Vice Chancellor, all right! He found skeletons in upstairs cupboards and threatened to expose a couple of dubious property deals a few years back when the university was buying up land for expansion. By April he had the VC and two other big cheeses eating out of his hand.'

'What's the connection with Culloden?' I ask.

'I was coming to that. The Professor's investigations into the alleged shady deals involved reference to a plot of land in Scotland, ostensibly for setting up a remote field station and weather observatory. Being naturally curious, he studied the background of the area in some detail and discovered a supposed link to the burial of large sums of money around the time of the 1745 rising. He realised that he couldn't do the whole operation on his own, and enlisted the aid of his Chief Technician in further exploration of several databases, one of which contained a snippet of information about a record in a lost book. It turned out that, unfortunately for the Professor, Joe blackmailed him into agreeing to a large share of the action.'

'Presumably, you knew what was going on because the Professor confided in you,' I say.

'I admit, he found me quite useful for digging around in libraries and book shops. Suffice it to say that he off-loaded onto me quite a lot. Enough to get me interested. After all, I do find it a bit of a dull life cooped up in an office all day, listening to everyone's grumbles.'

'So you struck a deal with the Professor?'

'Exactly. Get Joe off his back and take over his role in exchange for a modest, but quite reasonable share of the proceeds.'

Incensed, I address the Professor: 'Why did you have my keyboards contaminated with a narcotic and that bacillus?'

'He didn't intnd to kill,' Sadie interrupted. 'The afternoon before you started here, the Professor showed me a keyboard. It was yours, and - by courtesy of Joe who'd located the substances - he applied traces of the alkaloid narcotic to some of the keys. I didn't know what he was doing until afterwards. He put the keyboard back on your desk early next morning. The idea was make you feel compelled to use it and hence contact Hendrik more frequently. Joe was working with Hendrik who needed confirmation of your family links to the Jacobite gold. Hendrik got quite excited when he learned that a Miss Dow was being offered a post here. But Joe wanted to reduce the number of rival beneficiaries. And now two – ironically including him – are both dead!'

'What about the second contamination?' I ask.

'Joe repeated the process, ths time using another sample of his - more powerful, he said. But he didn't target you - he targeted me. All he had to do was apply the bacillus to a few of the most used keys to get me out of the way.'

'Then how did I end up with the infected one? I asked.

'He knows – ask him,' Sadie says.

The professor fidgets uneasily as he speaks to me: 'As Sadie's said, it wasn't intended for you, Lucy. You'll recall that there'd been problems with some staff workstations, including yours. That's why, as soon as he came in that morning, the first thing Joe did was a round of maintenance. He must have piled up everyone's keyboards together on the trolley. When he redistributed them, the infected one ended up on your desk – quite accidentally. It could have gone to any one of us! As it turned out, you got double trouble and Sadie got none.'

'The pair of you intended to kill him, though!' I say.

'No comment!' says Sadie. 'He died anyway, as you witnessed, in a most accident prone manner.'

Just then I hear a deep and familar voice from behind the closed door. 'This is Inspector Gordon Richards of Thames Valley Police. Put your weapon on the floor, Sadie Hart - NOW!'

I'm dumbstruck by the expression on Sadie's face. Unable to locate an exact target behind a closed door, she tries an alternative threat: 'Back off or the Prof gets it!'

She's crazy treating Prof as a hostage! I think. Then, pretending to alter my position to a more comfortable one in my chair, I carefully reach for the personal alarm attached to my hand bag.

Sadie glances in my direction: 'What d'you think you're doing, Lucy?'

I extract the pin.

The result is deafening. In the confusion that follows, the Professor sees his chance but fails to make the best use of it. He ends up with a bullet wound in his arm. But in the very instant that my alarm sounds, the door springs open to reveal a fully attired police officer with a firearm aimed in Sadie's direction. She leans forward and puts her gun on the floor.

I replace the pin to silence my alarm and the Inspector calls for an ambulance. The shock of all this won't hit me until half an hour later.

Meanwhile, I ask Inspector Richards, 'How did you know Sadie was armed?'

The Inspector nods to his Sergeant, who explains: 'We were alerted by Janet Croft, your cleaner. She was at the main entrance and called us as soon as she saw the situation unfolding on the security monitor.'

The officer passes the paramedics coming up the stairs.

'This way, chaps', calls the Inspector. 'Your patient Professor Hamilton is walking wounded in room B5.' Turning to Sadie, he adds: 'Miss Sadie Hart, I'm arresting you for having discharged a firearm with intent to endanger life. You do not have to say anything. But, it may harm your defence if you do not mention when questioned something which you later rely on in court. Anything you do say may be given in evidence. Take her to the car, Sergeant.' Turning to Professor Hamilton, he adds, 'And before you're discharged from hospital, I'd like a word with you, Professor.'

After the morning's events, I make my way to the refectory for a strong cup of coffee. My immediate concerns are for my job. What will happen next? Almost as if in answer, my mobile phone rings. It's the Inspector.

'Good morning, Lucy!' *First name terms - and he sounds jovial.*

'Hello Inspector, can you tell me if the case is closed yet?'

'That's what I'm ringing you about. Up until now we have one arrest. But this is only the beginning of our investigation. What I mentioned to you before still stands. OK?'

'Understood, Inspector,' I reassure him.

*****

Chapter 9

THE FOLLOWING DAY is Saturday and it's raining. No need to water my window box. A quick breakfast is followed by a session at my laptop. Now that Joe and maybe the Professor are out of the equation, I wonder when or if the promised computer updates will materialise. We may know by Tuesday next, as one outcome of Professor Hamilton's absence will be a visit from the Vice Chancellor - doubtless to include a departmental pep talk in the aftermath of recent events.

Meanwhile, there's one thing I can't get out of my head. Who can be the person mentioned by Hendrik? On the computer screen, my main heading is 'X' with a list of sub-headings:

Joe? Professor Hamilton? Sadie? Alison? Janet Croft? The VC - or one of his colleagues? Anyone else? For each of these I have 'M' for motive and 'I' for known involvement.

As an X candidate, Joe seems to have been eliminated by Inspector Richards. Could he be mistaken? I continue to scan the list. Alison? Surely not? Involvement, yes. On the scene helping me to tidy up after the raid on my home. Organising my treatment after contamination and informing the police. A trustworthy professional. what would be her motive? She must be earning at least four times my salary. I recalled the new Jaguar on her driveway.

What about Professor Hamilton? Maybe nearer three times my salary. But in his office confrontation Sadie had built a detailed case against him. His motive could be desire for fame as a leading figure in the unearthing of Jacobite gold.

Then there's Sadie herself - gun toting, agressive and impulsive. Why threaten Prof with a firearm? Would Hendrik have trusted her?

Next, Janet the cleaner. Kindly and considerate. But could this be a persona to hide a secretive 'X' role? Her earnings are no doubt minimal, which might prompt her to seek additional income.

The VC (or a close colleague). Possible involvement? Like most politicians, he would need to cover his tracks well to avoid scandal. Is this another reason why Hendrik was careful not to reveal the identity of 'X'?

Anyone else? Person(s) unknown; a posibility... All this is giving me brain-ache! 11.05am - I put the kettle on for some coffee.

No sooner do I raise the cup to my lips, when the doorbell rings. It's the Inspector. I pour him a cup as well and we sit at a table. Inspector Richards opens his folder and looks me straight in the eye.

'Lucy, what exactly were *you* doing in Prof Hamilton's office?'

'He called me in from my office along the corridor,' I say.

'Why did he want you in his office?'

'Perhaps he was prompted - being at gunpoint.'

'You're saying Sadie wanted you there?'

'I suppose so.'

'How much do you earn, Lucy?'

I tell him.

'Not much, is it?' he says, raising an eyebrow. 'On the other hand, you stand to gain a considerable amount in due course - if all goes well.'

'Do you think I was play-acting and set off my alarm just for fun? I was scared stiff.'

'My questions are routine. I have to ask them.' The Inspector's gaze rakes a piece of paper I'd brought to the table. 'Have you worked out who X is?' he asks.

'No. This is as far as I've got.' I reach acrosss to my desk and add two more sheets of scribble for Richards to scan. 'Perhaps you can help?' I say.

Silence, while he brandishes a pocket handkerchief and cleans his spectacles. 'Since our last meeting, I'm getting a little nearer and clearer, but not quite there yet. As Sadie and the Professor share the same pair of rooms, our search warrant enabled us to search through both sets of documents. Quite revealing. You remember your ill-fated ride in Joe's car?'

'I'm not likely to forget it - ever!' I say.

'Sorry to remind you. But the responses to our public notices included a dog walker near the crash site.'

'I didn't see anyone!'

'You wouldn't, it was two hours before the crash. The witness reported seeing a middle aged woman wrestling with a large rock on the dirt track and then covering it with leaves and grass. This was about twenty yards from from where the car left the track and plunged down the embankment. The witness filmed the woman's activities with her mobile phone and her images are a close match to Sadie. Not only that - we found a rough sketch of the crash site, with details of the rock and its camouflage, hidden away in Sadie's office filing cabinet.'

'You mean Sadie knew in advance that Joe's car was expected? So she tried to kill us both?'

'She claims she didn't know you'd be a passenger. But this conflicts with evidence from her and Joe's mobile phones.'

'She'd be aware of Joe's driving habits, though. Where was he planning to drive to? Was it the disused barn?"

'Yes, Lucy. Originally, you were to be handed over to someone else - whom I take to be X - in the barn.'

'You mean...'

'No doubt for execution. But the plan was changed - why not kill two birds with one stone and make it look like an accident?'

'One thing puzzles me,' I say. 'In this modified plan, why didn't X show up and make sure Joe and I were both dead?'

'To avoid risk of being noticed at the scene of the crime; and this could be accomplished by X deciding *not* to be near the scene - or the barn - allowing him or her to construct an alibi.'

'But what if Joe had managed to avoid skidding off the track?' I asked.

'One way or another, I believe you would have been by now a victim of murder.'

'Do you think I'm still in danger?'

'I think X has unfinished business and we need to act swiftly. That is the main reason for this visit.'

'I don't understand why X is still so active. The hoard has been located and at present is under guard. Surely there's nothing further to be done about it?'

'Unless there is more treasure to be found, Lucy. Don't forget, the university owns the land. How much of it I'm not sure, but I suspect that Professor Hamilton and the VC are keen to continue searching in case what has been found turns out to be the tip of an iceberg. And however limited your own claim may be, it would probably provide a significant income for life.'

'Whereas X wants to carry on reducing the number of potential beneficiaries.'

'Quite so.'

'It seems that Sadie wasn't happy with her share - hence the gun threat.'

'Yes, and all it achieved was attracting the interest of the police.'

'Another coffee, Inspector?'

'No thanks, I'd better be getting along. Look after yourself.'

I watch as the Inspector climbs into his squad car. Then I'm interested to see two plain clothed colleagues get out of the car, which drives off. The colleagues, a man and woman, take up positions at opposite ends of my street.

*****

Chapter 10

BACK AT WORK on the following Monday, I finish my coffee break to the sound of my phone. It's Alison.

'Sorry to ring you at work,' she says, 'but I'm just making sure that you're OK after all what you've been through these past days.'

'Well yes, thanks,' I say.

'Would you like to call in here on your way home today?'

An unexplained fear grips me. I pinch the end of my nose. 'That's very kind,' I say. 'But I've a real stinker of a cold coming on. Could we try Wednesday instead?'

'OK. You sound a bit rough. Catch up with you then. Bye.'

Phew! That should give me time to prepare myself, I thought. Perhaps I should update the Inspector.

His response surprises me: 'I was about to ring you. Avoid contact with anyone on your list. That includes postponing your visit to Alison. Simply don't turn up on Wednesday.'

'Can I ask why?'

'You can ask, Lucy. But I can't divulge police operations at this stage. I'll be in touch. Have a good day.'

On Wednesday evening I make myself a sandwich and turn on the TV for the news. Before anybody speaks I recognise Inspector Richards! He's being interviewed about two arrests he made earlier in the day.

'Sorry, I can't disclose suspect identities just now,' the Inspector says. 'All I can tell you is that they are a man and a woman, and that we are pursuing an enquiry concerning murder or attempted murder.'

'Is this in any way linked to the Jacobite gold find in Scotland?' asks the reporter.

'That's something we have to establish.'

'Or the cause of death in the recent car smash on Briar's Hill? We understand it was a nerve agent.'

'Yes, it did involve a nerve agent and decontamination is ongoing. It is still important for the public to avoid the cordoned area.'

'One more question, Inspector.'

'Yes, go on.'

'There was a police patrol car outside a surgery this morning. Is one of your arrested persons a nurse, receptionist or doctor?'

'Again, as I said, I'm not in a position to comment. Thank you.' The Inspector terminates the interview, brushes past the remaining paparazzi and leaves in his car.

I spend the rest of the evening unable to concentrate and I go to bed at 10.00pm - early for me - wondering about my friendship with Alison. Has it ended? I recollect the days we spent together when we were both students - and pull myself up with a start as a memory flashes by... a local fairground and its amusement arcade equipped with gambling machines. How she had a penchant - indeed an obsession - for one-armed bandits. Could it be that Alison is less well heeled than I thought? Is she plagued with gambling debts and looking for ways of paying them off?

After a night's fitful sleep I make some toast and coffee. The phone rings. It's the Inspector again. I glance at the wall clock, 6:25am - does he ever sleep?

'Hello Lucy, I know it's a bit early - can I come round?'

I agree to this and when he arrives I pour him some coffee as he relaxes on the sofa.

'I thought I'd better put you out of your misery in person,' he says. 'You've probably been awake all night thinking about your friend Alison.'

'Yes, you're right, ' I say. 'How did you know we're friends?'

'It's part of my job.'

I realise that he must have had access to her mobile phone calls, letters and other documents. 'I saw you on the local TV news last night,' I add.

'That's why I'm here, Lucy, on two counts. One, to tell you that I believe Professor Hamilton was referred to as X by Hendrik and he is now under arrest. And two, to let you know that Alison has been released without charge.'

My sense of relief must be obvious, but the Inspector's grim expression remains unchanged.

'She's very clever and has an excellent lawyer,' he says, 'so don't jump to any conclusions. I know it's going to be even more difficult for you now to observe while playing dumb.'

I feel as if I've hit the buffers. *What do I make of this? Do I take a long holiday away from it all?* As if reading my thoughts, the Inspector makes a suggestion:

'Now that you're on the road to recovery, why not resume your second visit to Scotland?'

'Yes, I'd like to visit the site at Watchman Hill near Elvanfoot.'

'Good. I'll have a word with Sheriff Carnegie and perhaps he can find you a place to stay. How long do you need?' Inspector Richards asks, rising from his chair.

'Thanks - just a couple of days, then Alison can sign me back to work.'

'In my view that may not be a good idea. When you're ready, get your hospital consultant to sign you back; I know Dr. Moran, ask him.'

The coach journey this time is more relaxed and I can enjoy the scenery. On arrival at Dungowrie I take a taxi ride to the bed and breakfast at Elvanfoot, kindly arranged by Sheriff Carnegie.

Next morning, after a hearty breakfast, I study the Sheriff's map given to me by the Inspector, check my packed lunch and set off on my six mile cross-country trek to the site of the hoard. The sun is shining and I'm down to my last sandwich, when I see the cordon tape in the middle distance. This reminds me of the TV newscast and the sight of the crumpled Shogun. I break out into a cold sweat. Poor Hendrik! As the tears roll down my face, one of the police officers sees me and begins walking in my direction.

'Hello. Can I assist?' she says. 'And who are you?'

I tell her who I am and she backs off in surprise. She calls her companion on her radio. I overhear the reply:

'Two Lucy Dows in one day - quite a coincidence, eh?'

I freeze and then fumble for my wallet in my rucksack. I show the policewoman my driving licence. She glances at my face and then my photograph.

'ID confirmed at this end, and the subject is distressed,' she reports. Turning to me, she asks: 'Are you OK?'

'Yes... I knew the driver of the car that crashed down that hole!'

'You'd better come with me,' she says, 'I'm Annie and that's Craig.' She nods in her colleague's direction. As we approach the cordon tapes I see that the person talking to Craig is Alison. *What on Earth is she up to?* I must be voicing my thoughts because Annie answers:

'D'ye know each other?'

'Yes, back in England she's my GP!'

'A Doctor, then,' says Craig. 'What's her real name?'

'Alison Ford,' I say.

60

Craig turns to Alison: 'What's the idea of you pretending to be someone else? You're very close to being booked for obstructing the police!'

'I'm sorry,' says Alison. 'I heared about the guy from Lucy and launched my own investigation. I needed to find a way of getting closer to the scene of the accident.'

'Accident?' says Craig. 'Incident might be a better description.'

'How do you mean, incident?' says Alison.

Not another one? The thought rings through my brain as I recall the gory details of Joe's car crash nearer home. A voice pulls me back to the present...

'Where were you on the seventh of June at 4.14pm?' Annie asks me.

'In the TV lounge of a B&B in Inverness,' I reply.

'And you, Alison - same question?'

'In my surgery 300 miles south of here,' says Alison.

'I had to ask these questions because it seems that Lars Petersen was joined by a female companion,' says Annie. 'Have either of you any idea who she might be?'

I give Alison time to respond. 'Not a clue!' she says.

'I believe Sadie Hart is in custody,' I say.

'Yes, we know about that,' says Annie.

Alison gives me a baleful stare while Annie edits some notes on her smart phone. Meanwhile, Craig walks around in figures of eight while calling up Sheriff Carnegie. Apart from that, I can't make out what's being said - except mention of 'brake fluid'. After the call, Craig addresses the whole group:

'There's been a forensic development. Sheriff Carnegie insists that no visitors to the site can enter the cordon. As of now, its radius is expanded by 100 yards. Alison and Lucy, could you please wait for me in the back of our patrol car? I'll be with you in a few minutes.'

In the car, I ask Alison the reason why she tried to use my name.

'I've already answered that question,' she says. 'I have nothing more to say.'

'Was it Sadie in the 4x4?'

'How on Earth should I know?'

'Did she do something to the brakes before they...'

'What the [expletive deleted] are you trying to involve me in?' Alison shouts.

At that moment, and much to my relief, Annie opens the driver's door, checks our seatbelts and starts the engine.

At Elvanfoot, we enter a car park and pull in next to a sleek black Jaguar. Annie photographs it with her smart phone. 'Doctor Ford, make sure you are available for interview at Thames Valley Police - and via video link with us if necessary,' she says.

'Yes.' is Alison's curt reply, before driving off.

'The same applies to you, Lucy.'

'Understood. And thanks for the lift.'

In the circumstances I have no regrets that Alison didn't offer me a lift back. I'd already booked and paid for my return coach journey. On arriving home I find a note from Inspector Richards, suggesting we meet. We agree a time over the phone and I make some more scones for him. At 7:15pm the doorbell rings.

'Hello, Lucy. You had a good journey back?'

'Yes, thanks. Time to think things through. Not that I'm any the wiser. How can I help?'

'You've probably heard that there is evidence of a female occupant in Hendrik's 4x4 - to use his alias name.'

'A passenger?'

'Not necessarily.'

'You mean, *she* was driving?' I ask.

'The forensics team found traces of brake fluid on Sadie's clothing, as if she'd wiped her hands after a spillage. The brake fluid formula matches that used in the 4x4 - or what was left of it.. And traces of the same fluid were found on the driver's seat, but none on the passenger seat. Yes, I think she was driving, at least for some of the time.'

'So she would know the brakes would fail, but Hendrik wouldn't. And if she was driving towards the hoard site, she could have jumped out of the vehicle before it encountered the hole.'

'Quite so. All conjecture of course. One difficulty is no seatbelts were being worn. That could assist Sadie's escape and in Hendrik's case be due to sheer excitement of the project. When his body was found, he could have been in either of the front seats before impact. But there is a possibility that the cracked windscreen on the passenger side was caused by his head, judging from hair samples... Sorry! Are you all right?'

I burst into tears. Again thinking of Hendrik and the evidence that he was another victim of heartless sabotage - all orchestrated by Sadie. But is that correct? Is she just a fixer with the plot being managed by someone else? Casting my mind back to Elvanfoot, the odds seem to stack up towards Alison as ring leader. I apologise and share these thoughts with the Inspector.

'Alison's arrival in Elvanfoot was interesting,' he says. 'I think she came to monitor the progress of our investigation. Either she's deeply involved in criminal activity or an amateur sleuth. I'm not sure which is worse! Anyhow, she nearly blew it when you appeared and confirmed your name to the local police... Er, thanks!' He takes another scone.

'There's something else you should know,' I say. 'When the policeman phoned the Sheriff, I may not have been the only one overhearing mention of brake fluid.'

'Really? I think this could be exactly what Alison needed to hear. We have to anticipate her next plan - and whether it involves Sadie.'

'What about Sadie?' I ask. 'Will she be allowed bail?'

'I reckon she's safer in custody, but my Chief disagrees. In fact, both Professor Hamilton and Sadie Hart will be bailed.'

'Do you think Alison could be seeking revenge on Sadie for bungling her task by leaving evidence behind?'

'Possibly. You've known her for some years - in your opinion is she capable of criminal intent?'

'I wouldn't know. She's good at her job, always very professional and helpful. Unpleasantly surprised on seeing me near the hoard site, but that's only to be expected, I suppose.'

'Well, Lucy, you have more justification in being near the hoard site than she has... hang on. What is it?' The Inspector answers his mobile phone. 'Oh! Hi there, Angus. About to burn the midnight oil, are we? How can I help?'

It's a call from the Inspector's working colleague in Scotland, Sheriff Carnegie. I top up the coffee and make sure the scones are in range. After a good five minutes they ring off.

'You'll gather, Lucy, that there's another witness to the 4x4 crash. In fact, two witnesses. Bird watchers with high power optics about a mile away. They saw a figure - presumably Sadie - take a flying leap from the vehicle before it disappeared. Angus has been busy pinning up notices everywhere appealing for witnesses. His efforts were rewarded about an hour ago!'

*****

Chapter 11

IN PROFESSOR HAMILTON'S absence, I hand my medical note from Dr. Moran to the Departmental Office and resume my research project in the ground floor laboratory. That's my intention. However, I'm interrupted by the vibrator on my smart phone.To my surprise it's Alison.

'Sorry again to bother you at work,' she says, 'but I owe you an apology for not offering you a lift from Scotland.'

I try not to be fazed but the words won't come.

'Lucy?' says Alison.

I pull myself together: 'Hi Alison. Is there anything else?'

'Yes, can we talk later? Could you arrive at 7.30 this evening at my place? You sound nervous; don't worry, some others will be coming.'

My mind is in turmoil, but curiosity wins: 'Very well Alison - be seeing you.'

I feel my heart thumping. Will this become a confrontation? I can't see it being a confession. My thoughts are interrupted by someone opening my office door. 'Hello, Janet!' I say.

'Hi Lucy. Glad to see you're back. If you like, I'll give your desk a wipe over. Would you like some coffee?'

'Yes, thanks, Janet,' I say absently.

Janet seems full of small talk, but I'm not in the mood for it. Soon, she leaves me with a shiny desk adorned with one fresh mug of coffee. *One mug?* I'm feeling paranoid with all that's been going during my first month in the job. *What is it laced with? And yes, she wore gloves.* I let the coffee go cold and decant a sample of it into a small bottle, washing its exterior and my hands in the laboratory sink. I now dispose of the remaining coffee and call the Inspector on my mobile phone. I explain the recent events, hoping I don't sound too insane.

To my surprise - and relief - Inspecor Richards responds with: 'I'll see you in your workplace later this morning and take your sample to Dr. Moran.'

The Inspector rings off and I feel so foolish. The sample is bound to test negative - and then what?

At 3.30pm he rings back: 'The test proved positive - the same bacillus that was used on the keyboards!'

I'm speechless. I break the silence by explaining that I have a meeting with Alison at 7.30pm.

'Yes, I'll be there, too - I've organised this with her. But it's important that you don't tell anybody.'

My head is spinning. 'Is anyone else coming?' I ask.

'Yes, I hope so. We have to move quickly now. Again, please keep this under your hat.'

I have half a mind to tell him I don't wear a hat - apart from my disguise worn in Scotland: 'Understood,' I say.

The familiar black Jaguar on Alison's driveway fills my field of view. I ease past it and ring the doorbell - invoking pleasant chimes.

'Great to see you!' Alison says. 'Come in and take a seat in the lounge.'

I find myself sitting opposite Janet Croft, who stares at me as if she's seen a ghost.

'Hi Janet! Thanks again for the nice desk job today and the coffee - I was so busy I forgot to drink it.'

Janet's facial expression becomes a brief scowl and she forces a smile: 'A pleasure, ' she says, 'and no problem.'

'Your coffee - actually, I had it analyzed,' I admitted.

'Then it won't surprise you that, like your personal alarm, I carry something around in my bag.' She reaches for it.

What follows in the next few moments is hard to convey. Firstly, a rustle from a hanging curtain behind Janet. She turns to face Inspector Richards. Next, a lithe figure in a tracksuit enters the room from the doorway, cartwheels swiftly past me and delivers a karate chop to Janet's right forearm.

'I'll take this,' says the Inspector, removing Janet's bag.

'Apologies!' says Alison, 'I don't normally treat my guests like this. Are you all right, Lucy?'

I'm dumbstruck, but nod in assent.

The Inspector opens Janet's bag and finds a loaded hypodermic. 'I'll have this examined as well,' he says. 'Meanwhile, Janet Croft, I'm arresting you on suspicion of attempted murder...'

'Two more guests arriving,' says Alison, as she glances through the window. She welcomes Professor Hamilton and Sadie Hart and ushers them into the lounge.

'Hello, Janet!' says the Professor, 'What are you doing here?'

'Being damn well arrested!'

'Oh! Are we all to share that fate?' he asks.

'Not necessarily,' says the Inspector. 'We're all here to tidy up a few loose ends. We'll begin with you, Professor. I understand you started this whole shebang by purchasing a tract of land in Scotland near Elvanfoot. Here are the authorizations, dates and costings of your enterprise - are they correct?'

'Yes, Inspector.'

'About the justification in your proposal - a weather station?'

'That's correct.'

'What about other personnel?

'Lars Petersen is - was - a journalist from Denmark.'

'With an interest in Scottish history, I understand.'

'We were both interested in the battle of Culloden.'

'And the reserve of hard cash to support the Jacobite cause?'

'Well, yes.'

'Did you work with Lars, otherwise known as Hendrik?

'Yes.'

'And you got on well with him?'

'Of course.'

'You threatened him, according to his records.' The Inspector hands the Professor a copy of Hendrik's final letter to Lucy and asks: 'Do you agree with the content of this?'

'We sometimes argued, like you do with colleagues.'

'If I treated any of my colleagues like that, I'd be out of the Force by my neck. Come now, Professor...'

'Alright, I was a bit short tempered sometimes, but I wouldn't have harmed him.'

'Quite so, you'd leave the harming to others.'

'What do you mean? This is outrageous!'

The inspector wheels round to face Janet. 'Miss Croft, you raised the alarm in the first instance, no doubt hoping that the Professor and Miss Hart would thereby be unable to profit from his enterprise.' Then he turns to Sadie: 'However, Miss Hart, who gave you the orders to sabotage the track on Briar's Hill and the brakes on Hendrik's 4x4 near Elvanfoot? Don't deny it - we have hard evidence for both.'

'It... it was Janet, Inspector.'

'Sadie! You [expletive deleted] bitch!' cries Janet.

'Well, time to close the circle,' the Inspector says, 'and Janet, who is pulling *your* strings?'

'Who do you [expletive deleted] - well think?'

With a nod from the Inspector, uniformed officers lead the Professor, Sadie and Janet to respective police cars outside the surgery.

A few weeks later after the trial, Alison asks me what I might do with the possible monies granted by the Treasure Trove Unit. 'A wee electric car would be fine,' I say.

*****

68

THE END

Printed in Great Britain
by Amazon

71785711R00047